STAR WARS

THE LAST JEDI

IN SEARCH OF THE
MASTER CODEBREAKER

ACT 2

Adapted by Michael Kogge

studio fun
INTERNATIONAL

On board the *Supremacy*, Kylo Ren kneels before Supreme
Leader Snoke surrounded by his lethal red-armored Praetorian
Guards. Snoke is doubting Kylo's potential and expresses his
disappointment by referring to him as merely a child with a
mask. Kylo is dismissed, furious at himself for not living up to
the legacy of his Vader bloodline and vows to prove himself
once and for all.

DISK 3

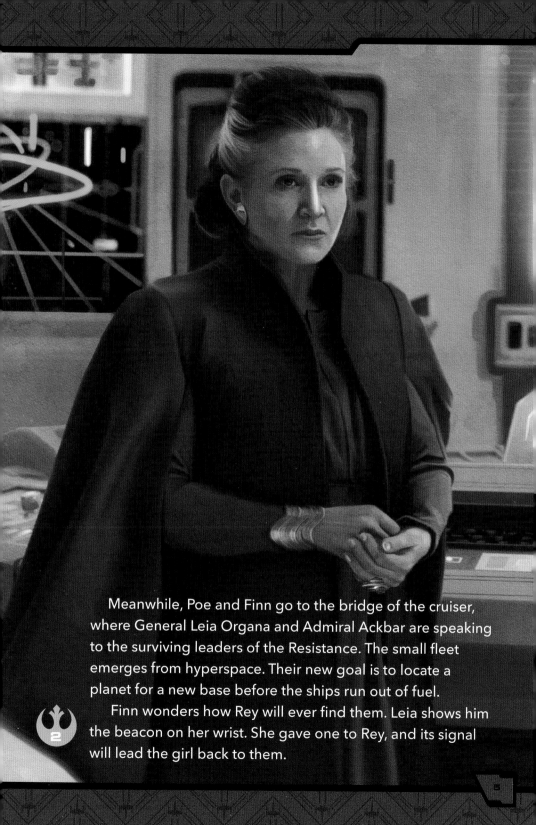

Meanwhile, Poe and Finn go to the bridge of the cruiser, where General Leia Organa and Admiral Ackbar are speaking to the surviving leaders of the Resistance. The small fleet emerges from hyperspace. Their new goal is to locate a planet for a new base before the ships run out of fuel.

Finn wonders how Rey will ever find them. Leia shows him the beacon on her wrist. She gave one to Rey, and its signal will lead the girl back to them.

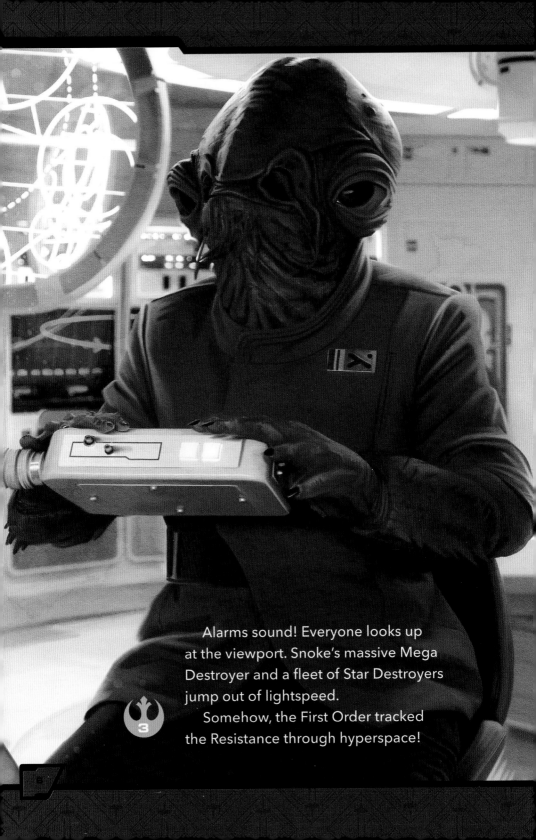

Alarms sound! Everyone looks up
at the viewport. Snoke's massive Mega
Destroyer and a fleet of Star Destroyers
jump out of lightspeed.
Somehow, the First Order tracked
the Resistance through hyperspace!

Poe, Finn, and BB-8 rush to help fight off the attack. The three split up, with Poe heading toward the hangar. Meanwhile, Kylo Ren speeds toward the Resistance cruiser in his own special starfighter. Several TIE fighters join him.

Poe doesn't make it to his X-wing in time. Kylo Ren fires torpedoes into the cruiser's hangar, destroying most of the Resistance starfighters, including Poe's X-wing!

On the bridge, Leia orders the ships in the Resistance fleet to raise their shields and push their engines to maximum power. They have to escape!

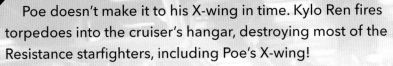

Finn sits down in a hallway. What can he do? He is trained as a stormtrooper, not a pilot. He will be no good out there blasting at TIE fighters—especially when he is worried about Rey.

BB-8 rolls by Finn. Noticing the young man seems sad, the droid projects a holographic recording. It shows Rey saying goodbye to an unconscious Finn before departing on her mission. He realizes he has to go find Rey.

Finn opens the hatch of an escape pod. A maintenance worker named Rose sees him and asks what he is doing. Finn can't explain himself. Rose figures he was a coward trying to run away from the battle. She takes a tool off her belt and fires a stun blast at him.

Meanwhile, Rey is determined not to leave Ahch-To without Luke Skywalker. She follows him to the tide pools where he milks the giant thala-sirens. She watches him spear fish off the cliff. She sleeps outside his hut in the cold and never leaves his side.

Through it all, Luke ignores her, not saying a word.

Later, Rey feels pulled toward a giant tree. She turns away from Luke and enters a hole in the trunk. The interior of the tree is hollow and has been made into a library. She approaches a shelf where a stack of books seems to have a slight glow.

Luke follows her inside. "Who *are* you?" he asks.

Rey reveals to Luke that she came from the distant planet of Jakku. For a long time, she has felt a power inside of her. Recently, it awakened to become even stronger. She needs an instructor to help her understand what it is and how to use it.

Rey's inner power is known as the Force. It is the energy that binds the galaxy together. In the days of the Old Republic, the Jedi called on the Force to do their extraordinary deeds and protect the galaxy.

Luke refuses to teach Rey in the ways of the Force, though. He came to Ahch-To so that all Jedi knowledge would die with him. He believes that it is time for the Jedi to end.

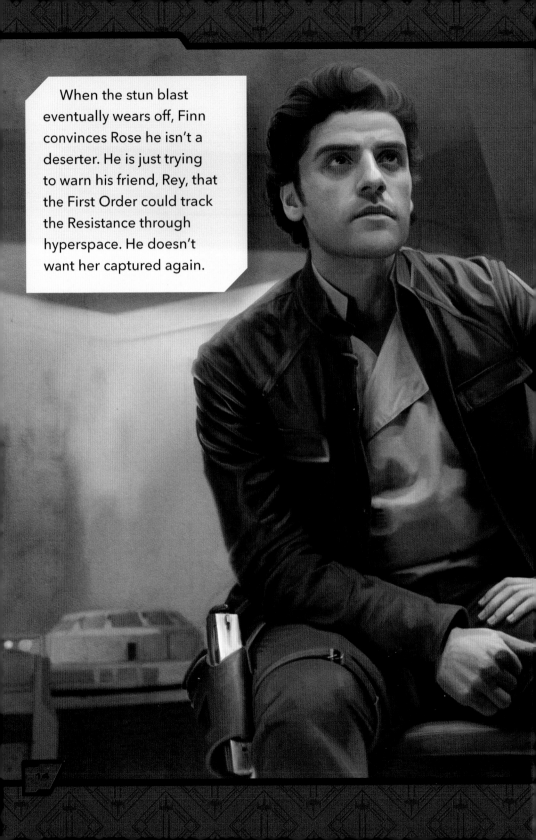

When the stun blast eventually wears off, Finn convinces Rose he isn't a deserter. He is just trying to warn his friend, Rey, that the First Order could track the Resistance through hyperspace. He doesn't want her captured again.

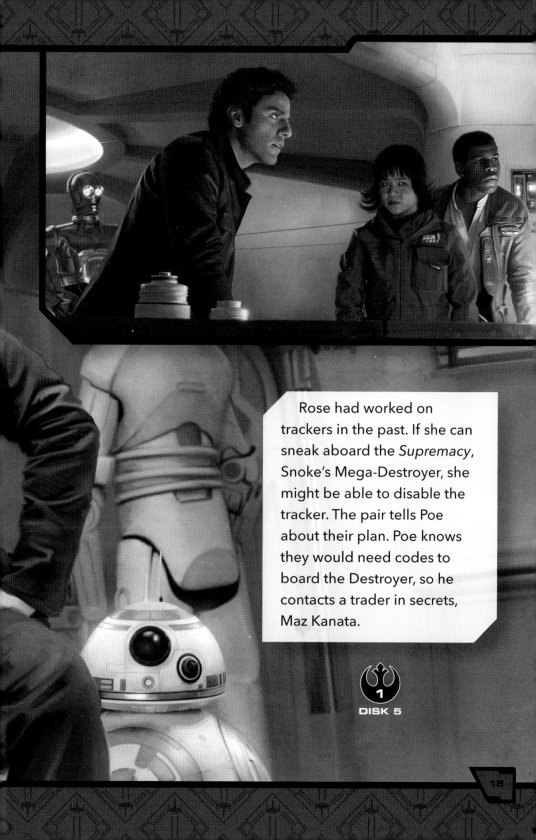

Rose had worked on trackers in the past. If she can sneak aboard the *Supremacy*, Snoke's Mega-Destroyer, she might be able to disable the tracker. The pair tells Poe about their plan. Poe knows they would need codes to board the Destroyer, so he contacts a trader in secrets, Maz Kanata.

DISK 5

Maz Kanata says the only person who can crack the codes for the *Supremacy* would be the Master Codebreaker. He lives in Canto Bight on Cantonica and likes to wear a red plom bloom flower below his collar.

Finn, Rose, and BB-8 travel to Canto Bight. The city's luxury hotels and casinos impress Finn. But he has no time for fun. If they don't find the Master Codebreaker soon, the First Order will catch the Resistance fleet and destroy it!

So Finn embarks on another adventure, searching for the Master Codebreaker with his new friend, Rose . . .

At night, Luke slips out of his hut. Neither Rey nor Chewbacca see him. Rey is fast asleep outside and Chewie is too busy growling at a flock of pesky porgs.

Luke walks up the ramp of the *Millennium Falcon* and snoops around. Seeing it again brings back memories. In his younger years, Luke flew aboard the *Falcon* on many adventures with his friends. One of those friends, R2-D2, beeps at him in the lounge.

The droid chirps that the Resistance needs Luke.
Though Luke is happy to see R2-D2 again, nothing can
change his mind.

R2-D2 then projects a hologram of a very young
Princess Leia, dressed all in white. She begged Obi-Wan
Kenobi to help the Rebel Alliance. Luke first saw that
hologram decades ago. At the time, he listened to Leia
and helped her.

Now he feels guilty.

R2-D2's hologram makes Luke reconsider what he should do. He goes to the bench in the village where Rey is sleeping. He tells her he'll teach her the ways of the Jedi— and why they need to end. But after their lessons are over, she has to agree she will leave him alone.

At dawn the next day, Rey and Luke begin their training.

Rey learns from Luke how to use a lightsaber and call on the Force, but she does not forget her mission. Despite what Luke said, she is not going to let General Organa down.
She will convince Luke to help save the Resistance—and the galaxy—from the evil First Order.